EDGE BOOKS

Epic Disasters

THE WORST TSUNAMIS OF ALL TIME

by Terri Dougherty

Consultant:
Susan L. Cutter, PhD
Director
Hazards and Vulnerability Research Institute
University of South Carolina

CAPSTONE PRESS
a capstone imprint

Edge Books are published by Capstone Press,
1710 Roe Crest Drive, North Mankato, Minnesota 56003.
www.capstonepub.com

Library of Congress Cataloging-in-Publication Data
Dougherty, Terri.
The worst tsunamis of all time / by Terri Dougherty.
p. cm.—(Edge books. Epic disasters)
Includes bibliographical references and index.
Summary: "Describes the worst tsunamis in history, as well as causes, types, and disaster tips"—Provided by publisher.
ISBN 978-1-4296-8416-3 (library binding)
ISBN 978-1-62065-221-3 (ebook PDF)
1. Tsunamis—History—Juvenile literature. 2. Ocean waves—Juvenile literature.
I. Title.
GC221.5.D68 2013
363.34'94—dc23 2011051839

Editorial Credits
Anthony Wacholtz, editor; Gene Bentdahl, designer; Marcie Spence, media researcher; Laura Manthe, production specialist

Photo Credits
Alamy: Asia File, 9, MPAK, 6; Brian Atwater, 27; Bridgeman Art Library: Look and Learn, 21; Corbis: 11, Baron Wilhelm Von Gloeden/National Geographic Society, 24–25, Bettmann, 14, 23, Xinhua, 8; Courtesy of Eiler Henrickson, 19; Getty Images: Hulton Archive, 13, Kazuhiro Nogi/AFP, 7, Nat Farbman/Time & Life Pictures, 17; iStockphoto: Reniw-Imagery, cover; Shutterstock: Arthur Eugene Preston, 28, Christian Vinces, 4, karamysh, 29

Printed in the United States of America in Stevens Point, Wisconsin.
012013 007152R

TABLE OF CONTENTS

WALL OF WATER

The ocean pulls far back from the beach. Fish flop on damp sand. In the distance, a giant wave grows. It heads toward land and surges onto the shore, flipping boats, pushing cars, and sweeping away homes. The water pulls back, but soon another giant wave bears down.

A tsunami is a series of large waves. The waves are created by a large **displacement** of water. The displacement can be caused by an earthquake, volcano, or landslide. The waves can move across the ocean as fast as a jet plane. Some waves travel at 400 to 600 miles (644 to 966 kilometers) per hour.

The fast-moving waves are not very tall in deep water. They are usually less than 3 feet (0.9 meter) high. A ship in deep water might not even know that a tsunami passed by. When the waves reach shallow water, however, the waves slow down and grow. They may be 10 times higher than they were in the deep ocean. They may tower more than 100 feet (30 m) high.

When a tsunami reaches the shore, it may look like a wall of water. It can also look as if the **tide** is quickly coming in or going out. Either way, a tsunami can bring a huge amount of water onshore in a short time.

After one tsunami wave hits the shore, the next wave usually follows in 15 or 30 minutes. But it may arrive in five minutes or take more than an hour to arrive. A shoreline may be pummeled by huge waves for several hours.

In a typical year, two tsunamis cause damage somewhere in the world. Most occur in the Pacific Ocean. About every 15 years, a major tsunami rolls across an entire ocean and causes major damage.

CAUSES OF TSUNAMIS

Tsunamis can be created in many ways. Earthquakes, landslides, and volcanoes are the most common causes.

Earthquakes: When huge pieces of Earth's crust move, underwater earthquakes can occur. The displaced water from the shift can create large waves.

Landslides: An earthquake may loosen a large amount of soil or rocks. When the soil and rocks fall into the ocean, they push the water and create a tsunami. Landslides can also occur underwater.

Volcanoes: The rocks and debris from an erupting underwater volcano in the ocean can create a tsunami.

displacement—the weight of water that is pushed away by an outside force such as a landslide
tide—the rising and falling of the ocean on the shore

JAPANESE TSUNAMI OF 2011

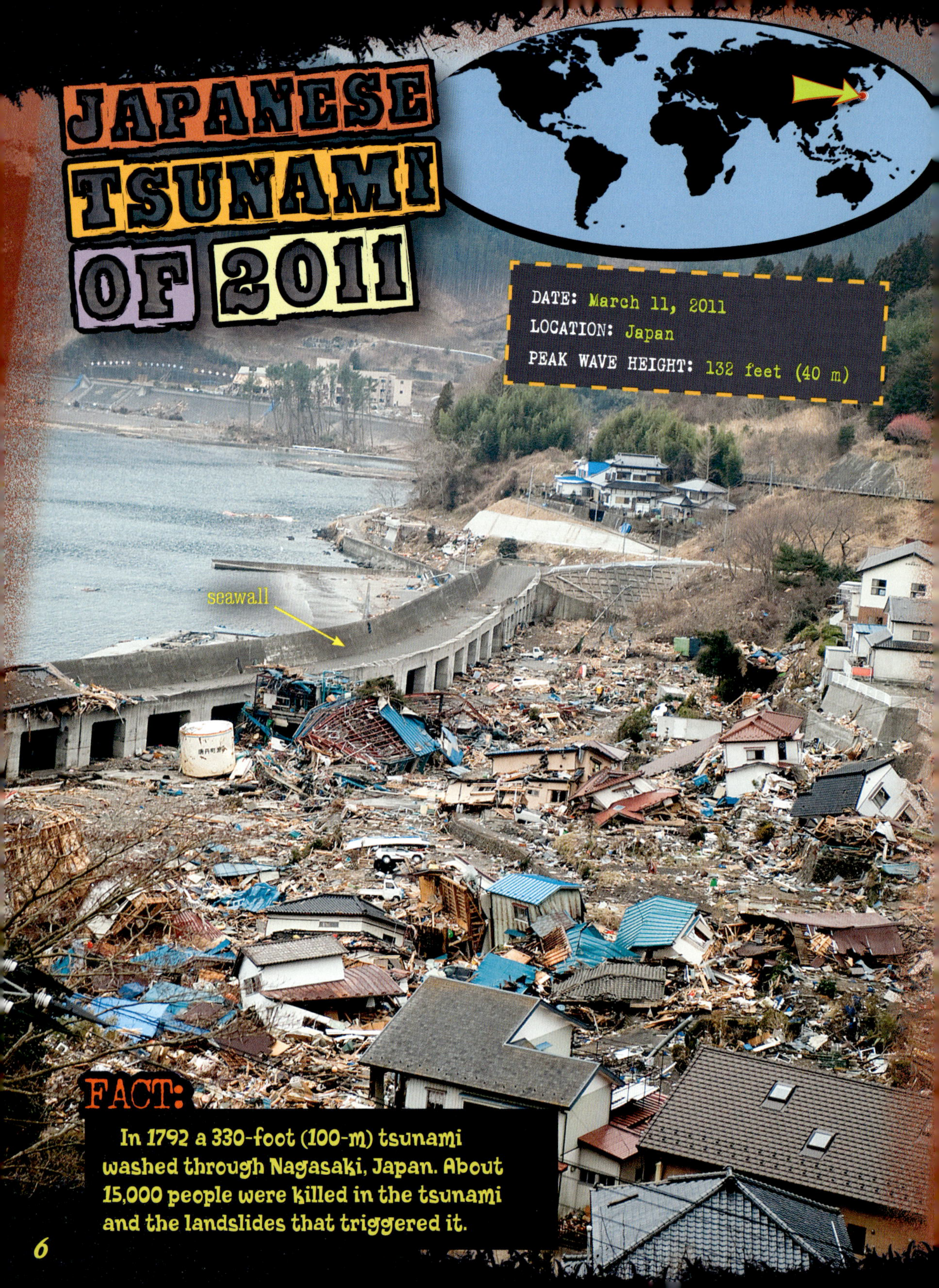

DATE: March 11, 2011

LOCATION: Japan

PEAK WAVE HEIGHT: 132 feet (40 m)

FACT:

In 1792 a 330-foot (100-m) tsunami washed through Nagasaki, Japan. About 15,000 people were killed in the tsunami and the landslides that triggered it.

A giant **seawall** was supposed to protect Kamaishi, Japan. But on March 11, 2011, a tsunami rolled over the wall and roared into the city. The rushing water tossed cars and crushed buildings. Streets became rivers filled with debris.

The scene was the same along the rest of Japan's northeast coast. Homes were ripped apart. Boats were shoved inland. A nuclear power plant was crippled.

The tsunami was caused by the strongest recorded earthquake to ever hit Japan. The earthquake occurred off of Japan's coast and measured 9 on the **Richter scale**. It created a tsunami that raced toward shore at about 500 miles (805 km) per hour. When it hit land, the wall of water was 132 feet (40 m) tall in some places.

In one city, people were saved by a stone tablet. The tablet in Aneyoshi, Japan, warned people not to build homes below it. The stone was put in place in 1896 after a tsunami washed over the village. People followed the stone's warning and were safe when the 2011 tsunami hit.

seawall—a structure built to protect land from waves and tides
Richter scale—a scale that measures the amount of energy in an earthquake; earthquakes with low numbers cause little or no damage

INDIAN OCEAN DISASTER

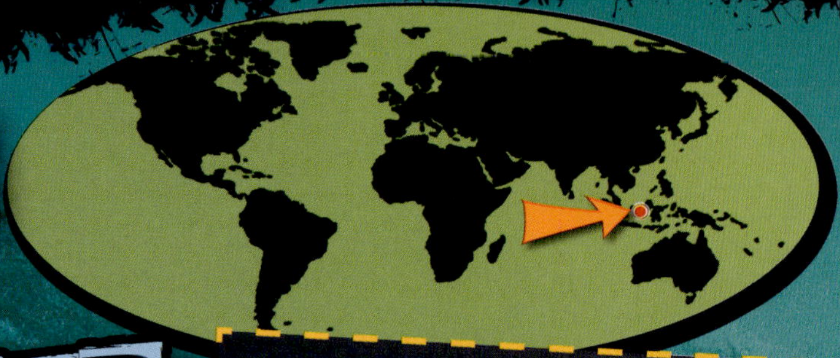

DATE: December 26, 2004

LOCATION: Indonesia and other Asian countries; Africa

PEAK WAVE HEIGHT: 100 feet (30 m)

A fisherman from Indonesia was on the water when he saw the sea draw back from the shore. Then he heard what sounded like bombs going off. Behind him, a giant wave was looming. It crashed down, throwing him from his boat. The wave dragged him toward the shore. He ended up on shore almost 2 miles (3.2 km) away. "It felt like doomsday," he said.

The fisherman lived through one of the world's worst tsunamis. The tsunami on December 26, 2004, was caused by an underwater earthquake west of Sumatra, Indonesia. The earthquake measured 9.1 on the Richter scale. It sent giant waves across the Indian Ocean. Huge waves washed over India, Sri Lanka, Thailand, and other countries. The waves were up to 100 feet (30 m) high. About 238,000 people were killed or missing, making it the deadliest tsunami in history.

FROM ALASKA TO HAWAII

DATE: April 1, 1946

LOCATION: Alaska, Hawaii, Pacific islands

PEAK WAVE HEIGHT: 115 feet (35 m)

The sturdy Scotch Cap lighthouse on Unimak Island, Alaska, had been built to withstand strong storms. Its base stood more than 40 feet (12 m) above **sea level**. However, even the concrete lighthouse was no match for a tsunami that hit the island on April 1, 1946. The tsunami began close to shore and hit the lighthouse soon after an earthquake. A wave 115 feet (35 m) high tore the lighthouse apart, leaving little behind.

The earthquake occurred just off the coast of Unimak Island. The powerful quake sent waves ripping across the Pacific Ocean. About five hours after it hit the Alaskan lighthouse, the tsunami reached Hawaii. A wave as high as 55 feet (17 m) crashed into the shore near the city of Hilo and surged inland. The city's waterfront was destroyed. The tsunami hit other islands in the Pacific Ocean as well, killing at least 165 people.

Many buildings were wiped out by the 1946 tsunami. Today engineers are working to limit the amount of damage a tsunami does to a building. Smaller waves would flow underneath buildings on stilts. Seawalls and groves of trees can also protect against tsunamis.

WARNING SYSTEM

The United States formed a tsunami warning center in Hawaii after the 1946 tsunami. The Pacific Tsunami Warning Center is on Ewa Beach on the island of Oahu. It sends tsunami warnings to islands in the Pacific Ocean and other countries around the world. There is also a Tsunami Warning Center in Alaska.

sea level—the level of the sea's surface

EXPLOSIVE TSUNAMI

DATE: August 27, 1883
LOCATION: Indonesia
PEAK WAVE HEIGHT: 140 feet (43 m)

Steam rising from the Krakatoa volcano hinted that something would happen. On August 27, 1883, a blast so powerful it was heard 2,800 miles (4,500 km) away blew the island apart. Ash spewed into the air and fell 520 miles (840 km) away. The explosion left only a third of the island remaining. But the massive eruption was not the only disaster. Soon after the powerful burst of **lava** hit the ocean, it created a towering tsunami. Waves up to 140 feet (43 m) high slammed into nearby coasts.

The islands of Java and Sumatra were hit hard by the tsunami. Krakatoa lies between the two islands. The tsunami wiped out 165 villages along the islands' coasts. The waves pushed a steamship 2 miles (3.2 km) inland and left it hung up on trees. The giant waves killed more than 36,000 people.

The tsunami waves then traveled across the Indian Ocean. Twelve hours after the tsunami hit Java and Sumatra, it reached the Arabian Peninsula. It had traveled 4,300 miles (6,920 km).

TAMBORA ERUPTION

The most powerful volcanic eruption ever recorded also created a tsunami. The Tambora volcano on Sumbawa Island, Indonesia, erupted in April 1815. The volcano spewed so much ash that the sky darkened. It created a tsunami that killed 4,600 people in the Indonesian islands.

lava—hot, melted rock that pours from a volcano

TERROR IN LISBON

DATE: November 1, 1755

LOCATION: Portugal, North Africa, Caribbean islands

PEAK WAVE HEIGHT: 50 feet (15 m)

On the morning of November 1, 1755, the earth shook under the Atlantic Ocean. The earthquake made Lisbon, Portugal, tremble. Homes and palaces wobbled. Stone buildings swayed and crumbled. Churches packed from All Saints Day services began to topple. People tried to get away from falling debris. They ran to the side of the Tagus River to avoid the falling buildings.

About 20 minutes after the earthquake began, another disaster roared toward the city. The earthquake had created a tsunami. A mountain of water surged inland from the sea and up the river. It lifted boats from their anchors and swept over the riverbank. The tsunami also damaged other cities along Portugal's coast. In some areas the waves were 50 feet (15 m) high.

The earthquake and tsunami were not the only disasters to hit Lisbon that day. Fires broke out and engulfed much of the city. A quarter of the people in the city died in the disaster. The combined disasters killed between 60,000 and 100,000 people.

After hitting Portugal, the giant waves spread out across the Atlantic Ocean, reaching North Africa and islands in the Caribbean. France, Great Britain, Belgium, and Holland were hit with smaller waves.

1964 ALASKAN TSUNAMI

DATE: March 27, 1964

LOCATION: Alaska, West Coast of United States and Canada

PEAK WAVE HEIGHT: 67 feet (20 m)

On March 27, 1964, one of the largest earthquakes ever recorded shook Prince William Sound, Alaska. The quake caused landslides that created about 20 tsunami waves. In Valdez a wave up to 67 feet (20 m) high destroyed the waterfront. Waves up to 30 feet (9.1 m) high smashed Kodiak's fishing boats.

One tsunami rolled across the Pacific Ocean. Under the light of the moon, four waves surged into Crescent City, California. The largest was 21 feet (6.4 m) high. It tossed piles of lumber into the air. A barge was pushed onto a dock. Buildings were torn from their foundations. The lighthouse keeper watched beds, mattresses, and TVs race by in the water.

The disasters were costly. The earthquake and tsunamis killed about 130 people and caused $311 million in damage.

TIMELINE

5:36 P.M.: An earthquake occurs off the coast of Alaska.

WITHIN A FEW MINUTES: Landslides cause tsunamis in the Gulf of Alaska.

THREE HOURS LATER: Tsunami waves wash over the coast of British Columbia, Canada.

FOUR HOURS LATER: A tsunami hits Washington, Oregon, and California.

FACT:

The 1964 Alaskan earthquake measured 9.2 on the Richter scale. It was the strongest ever recorded in North America.

THE LARGEST WAVE

DATE: July 9, 1958
LOCATION: Alaska
PEAK WAVE HEIGHT: 1,720 feet (524 m)

The largest tsunami wave ever recorded slammed across Lituya Bay, Alaska, on July 9, 1958. At 1,720 feet (524 m) high, it was taller than the Empire State Building.

The incredible wave formed when an earthquake caused a large chunk of rock to crash into the bay. The landslide created a powerful surge of water. The water hit a mountainside with such force that it ripped away the forest. Water rushed through the bay, tearing down trees and creating a barren landscape.

Several fishing boats were anchored in Lituya Bay when the massive tsunami struck. The wave lifted one boat more than 80 feet (24 m) high over trees and rocks. The boat was swept into the ocean, where it began to sink. A man and woman managed to get into a **skiff** and were rescued.

The anchor chain of a different boat broke. The boat was swept up to the top of the wave. It washed into the middle of the bay. Someone on the boat managed to steer around the debris in the water.

The tsunami tore down trees in an entire section of forest on the shore of Lituya Bay.

HIGH WAVES

In the early 1850s, a wave 395 feet (120 m) high tore through Lituya Bay. In 1936 a wave 490 feet (149 m) high tore trees from the sides of the mountains surrounding the bay. The bay often has large waves because it has deep water surrounded by steep slopes. It is also an area where earthquakes are common. Earthquakes can shake the rocks and ice loose on the side of the bay. The rocks and ice fall into the deep water, sometimes creating a tsunami.

skiff—a small rowboat

LOST CULTURE

DATE: around 1600 BC
LOCATION: Crete
PEAK WAVE HEIGHT: unknown

Four thousand years ago, the Minoans lived on the coast of Crete in the eastern Mediterranean Sea. They were known for creating beautiful art and grand buildings. Rulers lived in palaces. Their tidy towns included paved streets.

The Minoans traded with people on nearby Greek islands. They thrived for hundreds of years. Suddenly, the culture declined. Cities and palaces crumbled. No one knows exactly why this happened. Some scientists believe it was because of a tsunami.

A tsunami may have hit the island of Crete around 1600 BC. **Archaeologists** have found bits of pottery, cups, and animal bones mixed with shells and pebbles from the bottom of the sea. They were dumped high above sea level, out of the reach of storm waves. This discovery could prove that a tsunami crashed into the island. The waves may have left the Minoan culture in ruins.

archaeologist—a scientist who studies how people lived in the past

HUGE EARTHQUAKE, SURGING TSUNAMI

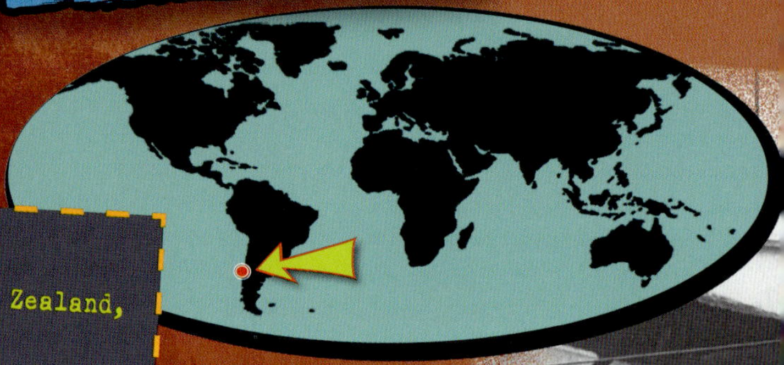

DATE: May 22, 1960

LOCATION: Chile, Hawaii, New Zealand, Australia, California, Japan

PEAK WAVE HEIGHT: 80 feet (24 m)

On May 22, 1960, the largest earthquake ever recorded rumbled off the coast of Chile. The earthquake measured 9.5 on the Richter scale. It created a tsunami that swept over Chile's coast. Wave after wave surged forward. The largest wave was 80 feet (24 m) high.

Tsunami waves also rolled across the Pacific Ocean. A wave 35 feet (11 m) high hit Hilo, Hawaii. Wooden buildings were crushed. Parking meters near the beach were bent. Rocks as heavy as 22 tons (20 metric tons) were tossed onto the shore.

High waves also hit New Zealand and Australia. Waves up to 5.5 feet (1.7 m) high damaged boats in California. Later 18-foot (5.5-m) waves came ashore in Japan. The waves hit **coral reefs**, causing the waves to bounce back across the ocean. It took days for the high waves to completely fade away.

TIMELINE

7:11 P.M.: An earthquake begins off the coast of Chile.

7:25 P.M.: Tsunami waves hit Chile's shore.

15 HOURS LATER: The tsunami reaches Hawaii, New Zealand, and Australia. The western coast of the United States is also hit by high waves.

22 HOURS LATER: The tsunami hits Japan.

Valdivia, Chile

coral reef—a type of land made up of the hardened bodies of corals

MESSINA TSUNAMI

DATE: December 28, 1908
LOCATION: Italy
PEAK WAVE HEIGHT: 39 feet (12 m)

On December 28, 1908, the people of Italy and Sicily were shocked by a double disaster. At about 5:20 a.m., a strong earthquake shook the area. It measured 7.2 on the Richter scale.

After the ground shook, a tsunami roared through the **Strait** of Messina. The narrow channel flows between Italy and the island of Sicily. The tsunami waves reached 39 feet (12 m) high. The waves crashed down on both sides of the strait, washing away houses and a railway bridge. Almost every building in the city of Messina was destroyed and almost half the people there were killed.

Scientists are not exactly sure how the tsunami began. Some experts think the earthquake created an underwater landslide in the Strait of Messina. The landslide shook loose more than 4.8 cubic miles (20 cubic kilometers) of rock. The rocks fell rapidly and could have created the tsunami. Other scientists think the bottom of the sea shifted during the earthquake and caused the tsunami.

Whatever triggered the tsunami, the results were devastating. The earthquake and tsunami killed between 70,000 and 110,000 people. They left towns and cities along both sides of the strait in ruins. Many who survived moved to the United States or other places after the disaster.

strait—a narrow channel connecting two large bodies of water

LOOKING BACK IN TIME

DATE: January 26, 1700
LOCATION: the Northwest and British Columbia, Canada
PEAK WAVE HEIGHT: unknown

In some ways the tsunami that followed the Great Cascadia earthquake is a mystery. Records show that a 9.0-magnitude earthquake rocked the northwestern U.S. coast and Canada on January 26, 1700. But no one wrote down anything about a giant wave hitting the western coast of North America following the earthquake. However, the tsunami left several clues that helped scientists learn more about it.

Scientists have found sand under the soil of the coast from northern California to British Columbia, Canada. They think the sand was carried there by a tsunami.

Trees along the coast also point to a tsunami. Scientists dug up trees that had died in the area. They looked at the **growth rings** in the tree stumps to find out when they had died. The scientists believe something killed the trees in 1700.

growth ring—a layer of wood produced by trees each year

Scientists also learned that a tsunami struck Japan on January 27, 1700. Waves 16 feet (4.9 m) high soaked the coast. Japanese writers recorded the day it came ashore.

Scientists guess that an earthquake likely caused the tsunami. However, Japanese writers did not say anything about the ground shaking. Neither did writers from other places where earthquakes often occur. This lack of evidence makes scientists think the earthquake happened close to North America. They believe it occurred in the Pacific Ocean near the western coast of North America.

a computer simulation of the 1700 tsunami waves

FACT:

Scientists think the earthquake happened at about 9:00 p.m. on January 26, 1700. They based the date on how long it would take the waves to travel to Japan.

LIVING WITH TSUNAMIS

To help keep people safe from tsunamis, scientists monitor earthquakes and the ocean. When an earthquake is detected, they determine if the quake might create a tsunami. **Buoys** in the ocean and **tide gauges** on coasts measure wave height. The information goes to scientists at tsunami warning centers.

At a warning center, computer programs help scientists predict where and when a tsunami will come ashore. The programs also help scientists determine how high waves will probably be when they hit the coast.

When an area is in danger of being hit by a tsunami, a warning is given. A siren may sound along the beach. TV and radio stations will broadcast the warning. They will give information about a safe way to leave the area. People need to leave the coast for higher ground.

If a tsunami is created by a distant earthquake, the waves may take several hours to hit the shore. But don't watch for a tsunami from the beach. When the wave can be seen, it is too late to outrun it. The water will recede and then rise rapidly when a tsunami hits.

If a tsunami is created close to land, people have little time to take action. The tsunami may arrive in less than half an hour. If an earthquake is felt, you should leave the shore quickly. Don't wait for an official warning to be issued. If roads have been cracked by the earthquake, get to the upper floor of a sturdy building. As a last resort, climb a tree to get above the waves.

If you live near an ocean, get to higher ground if any of these warning signs occur:

- intense shaking, usually lasting more than 20 seconds
- an earthquake that is strong enough to knock people off their feet
- water withdrawing in the sea
- a loud booming noise or roar like an oncoming train

buoy—a floating object anchored to the bottom of the ocean that can be used to measure wave height
tide gauge—equipment that measures water depth and the rise and fall of tides

GLOSSARY

archaeologist (ahr-kee-AH-luh-jist)—a scientist who studies how people lived in the past

buoy (BOO-ee)—a floating object anchored to the bottom of the ocean that can be used to measure wave height

coral reef (KOR-uhl REEF)—a type of land made up of the hardened bodies of sea creatures called corals

debris (duh-BREE)—the remains of something that has been destroyed

displacement (diss-PLAYSS-muhnt)—the weight of water that is pushed away by an outside force such as a landslide

growth ring (GROHTH RING)—a layer of wood produced by trees each year

lava (LAH-va)—hot, melted rock that pours from a volcano

Richter scale (RIK-tuhr SKALE)—a scale that measures the amount of energy in an earthquake; earthquakes with low numbers cause little or no damage

sea level (SEE LEVL)—the level of the surface of the sea

seawall (SEE-wahl)—a structure built to protect land from waves and tides

skiff (SKIF)—a small boat with a flat bottom

strait (STRAYHT)—a channel linking two bodies of water

tide (TIDE)—the rising and falling of the ocean on the shore; there are usually two high tides and two low tides in one day

tide gauge (TIHD GAYHG)—equipment that measures water depth and the rise and fall of tides near shore

READ MORE

Cunningham, Kevin. *Surviving Tsunamis.* Children's True Stories: Natural Disasters. Chicago: Raintree, 2012.

Higgins, Nadia. *It's a Tsunami.* Weather Watchers. Edina, Minn.: Magic Wagon, 2010.

Lace, William W. *The Indian Ocean Tsunami of 2004.* New York: Chelsea House Publishers, 2008.

Levy, Janey. *World's Worst Tsunamis.* Deadly Disasters. New York: PowerKids Press, 2009.

INTERNET SITES

FactHound offers a safe, fun way to find Internet sites related to this book. All of the sites on FactHound have been researched by our staff.

Here's all you do:

Visit *www.facthound.com*

Type in this code: 9781429684163

INDEX